Gwen

Lucky Girl

Editorial Director: Marge Kennedy
Retold by John W. Kennedy
Based on Ben 10 Episode #10 by Marsha Griffin

little monks on the wisdom tree

The Tennysons are levitated by the evil sorcerer Hex.

Hex seeks control of *The Arcameda Book of Spells.*

CHAPTER ONE:
The Arcameda Book of Spells

The gloom of night had already descended on New Orleans when the tour of the Museum of Witchcraft got underway.

A mysterious old woman who seemed to know even more than she was telling was leading the group of seven tourists through the cavernous repository.

"...and behind this impenetrable glass," she lectured, "is the recently discovered, and only known copy of, *The Arcameda Book of Spells.*"

The air took on a strange chill as she spoke.

"It contains," she continued, "ancient witchcraft..."

"...and rituals from the late 1600s," a young girl's voice chimed in.

The annoyed tour guide looked in the direction of the 10-year-old redheaded girl who had the audacity to interrupt her.

"And what's *your* name, young lady?" the old woman asked with a hint of disdain in her voice.

"Gwen Tennyson," the girl replied.

"Maybe you should work here, dear," the aged tour guide said.

A tiny smattering of nervous laughter emanated from the tour group and echoed down the hall.

"Don't let 'Mummy Face' get to you," whispered Gwen's cousin Ben, who was also 10-years-old. "She's probably older than that spell book," he added to Gwen's laughter.

"Shhh," Grandpa Max scolded.

There wasn't much that could scare Gwen or Ben. They had seen so much since they began their summer-long road trip in Grandpa Max's beat-up Recreational Vehilce (RV), Rustbucket.

It all began with Ben coming into contact with a strange wristwatch-like device called the Omnitrix during a campout in the woods. The device attached itself to his wrist, linking his DNA to that of superheroes from all over the universe.

In the months that followed, the trio had

fought several intergalactic villains and even a sea monster. So fear was not a problem for Gwen.

In fact, the hardest part of the summer was watching her cousin – the new superhero – take all the bows for defeating the weird bad guys even though she knew she was as brave and capable as he was. She didn't actually hold it against Ben. She just wished for a share of the spotlight.

As the tour continued, the group's trek down a long dark corridor was interrupted by an eerie humming sound. Suddenly everyone, including the ill-humored tour guide, began mysteriously floating toward the high ceiling. Upward they drifted until they were all pinned to the wood-beamed roof.

While the others screamed in panic, the Tennysons and their guide remained silent.

It was as though the old guide was used to being levitated. And as for the Tennysons, floating in the air was less scary than battling aliens from outer space.

Still, even for them, this wasn't ordinary.

"Something tells me this isn't a planned part of the tour," Grandpa Max quipped.

Then a crimson-red mist penetrated the museum's stained-glass skylight and began spinning around in a mesmerizing circular motion.

It appeared to be looking for something.

The horrified spectators looked on as the unearthly cloud descended toward the glass encasement holding *The Arcameda Book of Spells*.

Before their eyes, the haze began taking shape. As it magically solidified, it took the form of a man – a skeletal figure wearing a black hood with scarlet trim. He held a walking stick hewn into the shape of a snake with a vulture's head. Around his neck were five bejeweled charms, each emitting a visible energy field.

"*Taraka avendu!*" the spectral being pronounced as the encasement around the book shattered. The book then floated into the sorcerer's hands.

Gwen watched as Ben quietly reached for his Omnitrix. If there was ever a time to "go hero," this was it.

But the inscrutable hooded man seemed to

sense the young superhero's intention. As he turned around and looked up at his hovering hostages, he suddenly released them, causing his terrified captives to fall toward the floor.

As their screams echoed though the hall, Ben transformed into...XLR8!

Acting with only a second to spare, the superfast alien from planet Kinet raced to grab the large hanging museum banner. He tied its ends, creating a giant canopy to break everyone's fall and slide them gently to the ground.

"Everyone out!" XLR8 commanded. Not knowing whether to be more afraid of their captor or their rescuer, they complied.

"Ben, be careful!" Grandpa Max warned as he assisted people to the exit. "You don't know what tricks he's got up his sleeve!"

XLR8 turned to face his mysterious adversary.

"Dude," he taunted, "you want a book? Try the library!"

The interloper then stared at XLR8 and chanted, "*Venti mordal natta!*"

Immediately, flames encircled XLR8 and set fire to the museum! XLR8 ran in a circle, creating enough wind to put out the inferno.

The shadowy magician responded by lifting his walking stick and shooting out a beam of kinetic energy that honed in on XLR8. As it struck, it delivered an electrical wallop that stunned the alien hero and brought him to the ground.

Thinking fast, Gwen and Grandpa Max tipped over a pair of garbage cans and rolled them toward the evil spellcaster, knocking him over. As he got up, he turned toward them and scowled.

"I guess we got his attention," Gwen said.

"I kinda wish we hadn't," Grandpa Max retorted wryly.

The sorcerer's icy stare created an energy force that pushed Gwen and Grandpa Max backward and made it hard for them to breathe.

Just as they were about to pass out, XLR8 revived. With superfast speed, he began to circle the wicked warlock, creating a vortex that somehow disabled his supernatural powers. As XLR8 repeatedly punched him, the vile villain became increasingly dizzy.

The once seemingly all-powerful foe toppled helplessly to the floor. The impact dislodged one of the amulets from his necklace. As the charm rolled away, XLR8 picked it up as a souvenir of his victory.

"Nice job," Grandpa Max commended while looking down at the unconscious miscreant.

"Just doing what I need to do and keeping it low key," XLR8 replied with mock humility.

Of course, it wasn't long before the local media arrived, and Ben, still in the form of XLR8, was only too pleased to pose for pictures.

"Who's your hero?!" the immodest superhero shouted, stumbling upon his new catchphrase.

Gwen could only roll her eyes as her cousin Ben once again soaked up all the available glory.

CHAPTER TWO:
A Gift for Gwen

Later, as Grandpa Max drove the Rustbucket toward a nearby Cajun restaurant, Gwen and Ben sat at the table, watching TV news.

"Earlier this evening," the anchorwoman began, "the mad magician, who New Orleans residents know as 'Hex,' made a brazen attempt to steal *The Arcameda Book of Spells* from the Museum of Witchcraft.

"Using his power of levitation," she continued, "the sorcerer held several museum-goers, as well as a tour guide, in his evil grip while he broke through the glass containing the magic text.

"But before he could get away," she went on, "the alien hero XLR8 arrived on the scene to battle the warlock and save the day."

Then, over a video clip of XLR8 taking his bows, she concluded, "Here he is accepting the gratitude of a happy public."

Having heard enough, Gwen hit the remote and shut off the set.

"Hey! I was watching that!" Ben barked at his cousin.

"What kind of reporter is she, anyway?" Gwen complained. "I thought journalists were supposed to be objective."

"What's your problem?" Ben shot back. "XLR8 is a hero – which means I'm a hero. That was a fair report – end of story."

"Fine, you're a hero" Gwen conceded, "but all I'm saying is you didn't exactly stop that creep all by yourself today. I helped save your sorry butt. But does anybody notice *me*?"

"Hey," Ben responded, "being a hero is not about getting attention, right, Grandpa?"

"I noticed you, Gwen," Grandpa Max said.

"Thanks," answered Gwen, "but we're related. That doesn't count."

"No offense," Ben pressed, "but you threw a trash can at the guy. I'm the superhero who actually brought him down."

"Will you wake up!" Gwen shouted back.

"The only reason you're a 'big hero' is because of that watch. If I found it instead of you, I'd be getting all the attention and all the cool souvenirs!"

Though he didn't want to admit it, Ben knew there was truth to what Gwen said. So he reached into his box of mementos and pulled out the charm that had fallen off Hex's necklace during their battle.

"Here, take this," he offered as he handed her the gem.

"Really?" smiled Gwen.

"Yeah," he answered. "I got other stuff."

She reached out and grabbed the charm tightly in her hand.

"Gwen," Grandpa Max interjected, "don't you have something you want to say to Ben?"

She looked at her cousin as he awaited her declaration of appreciation.

"You know," she noted, "this doesn't change the fact that you're a hero because you're lucky – but thanks."

"You're welcome," Ben replied, feeling strangely good about being nice to his cousin Gwen.

Meanwhile, as the ambulance carrying the unconscious Hex neared the local hospital, the medical monitoring equipment he was hooked up to began beeping erratically.

The straps holding Hex to his gurney suddenly snapped, and the ambulance's rear doors swung open. Then his body levitated toward the exit. The ambulance driver and medic stared in disbelief.

"My destiny shall be fulfilled!" Hex declared as he floated outside and disappeared into the night.

Just a short distance away, the Tennysons were finally settling in for a genuine Cajun dinner – including Grandpa Max's favorite recipe, Louisiana Crawfish Boil, featuring a healthy helping of live crawfish! The critters scampered across hungry patron's plates.

At first, being city kids, the idea of eating anything that was still moving really grossed Gwen and Ben out. But, as they got into it, they understood why Grandpa Max had gone on so much about the dish.

In fact, the two cousins even found themselves

competing to see who could down more of the twitching delicacies.

"Hey!" Gwen complained. "You've eaten eleven crawfish, and I've only had nine!"

"So I guess it's time to make it an even dozen," Ben quipped as he went to spear the last crawfish with his fork.

But Gwen wasn't giving up without a fight. She knocked Ben's hand aside, causing him to lose his grip on his fork, which flew out of his hand, fell to the floor, and jabbed the busy waitress in the foot.

"*Yowch!*" she screamed as she threw her tray into the air, sending a drinking glass hurtling upward toward a spinning chandelier, which catapulted it into the kitchen, where it hit the chef, causing him to bump into the food cart containing a stack of uncooked crawfish!

The cart then rolled out into the dining area and straight at the Tennysons' table, and the entire pile of crawfish landed on Ben's head!

Before Ben could even process that weird chain of events, one of the crawfish climbed up his nostril, causing him to sneeze it out.

Gwen and Grandpa Max both enjoyed a big laugh. Ben, however, was not amused. He hated looking ridiculous.

As Ben wiped his nose, Gwen noticed a strange glow coming from her new lucky charm as it dangled from her necklace.

Meanwhile, back at the Museum of Witchcraft, Hex was on a rampage, holding the security guards upside-down in midair.

"*The Arcameda Book of Spells,*" he demanded, "where is it?"

"We locked it in the vault," one of the helpless guards confessed as he pointed Hex in the direction of a huge vault.

Hex stared at the safe. As he concentrated, the building shook with a supernatural energy.

Within moments, the heavy steel box was torn from the wall.

"*Badar avivimo norata!*" Hex thundered, commanding the safe's 10-inch-thick door to fall off its hinges.

Then *The Arcameda Book of Spells* floated toward Hex's waiting hands. But instead of catching the tome, he suspended it in flight, levitating it in front of himself as he turned its pages with a wave of his hand.

Finding the page he wanted, he gloated, "Yes, soon my powers will know no limits!"

Hex and *The Arcameda Book of Spells* began to glow as the mad sorcerer harnessed its energy. But after reaching a certain level of high intensity, the power began to dissipate.

"One of my charms is missing," Hex realized. "Without it, I cannot harness the full power of *The Arcameda Book of Spells!*"

Hex thought back to the day's events.

"That speed creature must have taken it," he deduced. "I must retrieve it!"

Hex once again transformed himself into a scarlet-red mist and wafted away in search of the missing jewel.

CHAPTER THREE:
Lucky Girl to the Rescue!

After their crawfish meal, the Tennysons went for an after-dinner stroll down a French Quarter side street.

"You know, in all my travels," Grandpa Max chuckled, "I've never actually *seen* a crawfish climb up into someone's nose – at least not until tonight."

Gwen and Grandpa Max then laughed again as the image of Ben sneezing out a crawfish replayed in their minds.

"I'm glad I could make your day," Ben said sarcastically.

"Don't let us bother you," Grandpa Max advised. "Everyone's on the receiving end of humor sometime. The best thing to do is join in the fun and develop the ability to laugh at yourself."

"*Ha ha!*" Ben said unconvincingly.

"By the way," Gwen said, "thanks for the charm.

"You earned it," Ben acknowledged.

Acting on that impulse, Gwen ran up to a corner hotdog vendor, took out her purse, and said, "One, please."

But before the vendor could fulfill her order, Gwen, Ben, and Grandpa Max heard a scream from just a few feet away.

"*Help!*" the voice of an elderly Southern belle cried out. "They stole my purse!"

As the Tennysons looked in her direction, they saw three street punks heading down the street.

Grandpa Max stepped in the middle of the sidewalk to confront them.

"That's far enough," he commanded.

The hoods stopped, but they weren't intimidated.

"Yeah?" the leader challenged, brandishing a metal pipe. "Who's gonna stop us? You, Pops?"

"Yeah," one of the other crooks echoed. "Who's the old man think he is?"

As Gwen stood with Grandpa Max, Ben ducked behind the hotdog cart and pressed down on his Omnitrix. But nothing happened.

"C'mon! *Work!*" He pounded the watch again. "Oh, boy," he whispered to himself. "This isn't my lucky day."

"Hey, that's a nice necklace you get there, little girl," the third punk said to Gwen as he reached for the jewel.

As Gwen took a step back, the charm on her necklace again began to glow.

She then accidentally bumped into a passing juggler who was riding by on a unicycle. The juggler fell down, sending his unicycle flying into one of the punks, knocking him out. Meanwhile, one of the bowling pins he was juggling landed on the head of the gang's leader, causing him to fall into Grandpa Max's arms.

While watching the bizarre sequence of events, the hotdog vendor unwittingly knocked his mustard dispenser to the street: Gwen inadvertently stepped on it, squishing the mustard into the face of the vendor, whose stunned reaction led him to release his cart, which crashed into the last punk, trapping him against the wall.

And for good measure, the resulting vibration

caused a flower pot that was sitting on the railing of an apartment terrace to teeter and land on the head of the other goon just as he was waking up.

Within seconds, the police were on the scene, and the old woman was expressing her gratitude to Gwen.

"Officer, this little girl is a hero!" the old woman gushed. "You should have seen the way she stepped up to fight those criminals."

The woman then took back her stolen purse, reached into it, and pulled out $50.

"Here," she offered Gwen, "take this as a reward."

"No, thank you," Gwen answered. "Helping you get your purse back is reward enough for me."

"You *are* my hero," the old woman smiled.

"I'm just lucky," Gwen smiled back as she rubbed her still-glowing charm.

"And you, young man," the woman said as she looked down at Ben, "I don't blame you for hiding behind the cart. Those ruffians were dangerous. You must feel so lucky to have such a heroic sister."

"Actually, I'm his cousin," Gwen said.

As the police tossed the young hoods into their police van, the old woman went on her way.

"Nice work, Gwen," Grandpa Max said. "Well, this has been quite a night. What do you say we all head back to the Rustbucket and get some shut-eye?"

"I'm for *anything* that will get this night over with," Ben groaned.

But Gwen, catching sight of some Halloween-type masks and costumes being sold at a stand across the street, had another idea.

"Grandpa Max," she asked, "would it be okay with you if I checked out the outfits?'

"Sure, why not?" Grandpa Max replied. "You've certainly earned it."

The next morning, with the glare of the rising sun shining through his window, Ben awoke to the sound of a jackhammer.

But a glance toward Grandpa Max's bed revealed that it was merely his grandfather's industrial-strength snoring that was making the racket.

Ben covered his head with his pillow. He tried to roll over and go back to sleep, but it was no use. He felt like he was trying to sleep inside a tooth while a dentist was at work fixing a cavity.

"Hey, Gwen," Ben cried out, "do you have a mega-sized cork on you?" But there was no answer.

"You can't possibly be sleeping through this, can you?" he asked while glancing down at the lower bunk.

But to Ben's surprise, Gwen was gone from her bed.

"Gwen, where are you?" he called out.

Then, in between Grandpa Max's snores, he heard the faint sound of a dribbling basketball.

As he stepped outside, he saw some guys getting ready for work, but no sign of Gwen.

Then more dribbling. He looked to his right and spotted his cousin with her back to a regulation 10-foot-high basketball hoop.

She was dribbling a basketball as her neck charm once again began to glow. She then hurled the ball back over her head toward the net. But her aim was too high, and the ball went soaring over the backboard.

XLR8 battles Hex.

"Who's your hero?!"

Gwen receives her lucky charm.

Lucky Girl to the rescue!

Wildmutt watches as Lucky Girl takes the bows.

Hex sees Lucky Girl on TV!

Two Tennyson superheroes is one too many for Ben.

Gwen and Ben race to save the day.

However, her shot was just beginning. The basketball then bounced off the roof of the Rustbucket, ricocheting off its TV antenna. The antenna then acted like a spring, shooting the ball toward a telephone pole. It then bounced off the pole and landed atop phone wires. From there, it rolled along like a circus acrobat performing a high-wire act.

The orange orb then spun its way over the basketball net, where it wavered for a few seconds before swishing its way through the hoop.

Score!

"*Yes!*" Gwen sang. "Nothin' but the bottom of the net again!"

"How'd you *do* that?" Ben asked, reluctantly impressed as he caught the ball.

"Gimme that back," Gwen demanded.

"Not till you tell me how you made that shot."

"What can I say? I'm charmed."

At that moment, the charm on her necklace glowed brighter before resuming its normal state once again.

"What did that thing just do?" Ben asked.

"I don't know," Gwen replied, "but every time it glows, everything just goes my way."

Then the door of the Rustbucket swung open.

"There you kids are!" Grandpa Max boomed, happy after a good night's sleep. "Who wants breakfast?!"

Before Gwen and Ben could answer, they heard the sound of men screaming behind them. They turned around and saw an out-of-control crane ramming into the partially constructed building. The impact snapped some safety cables tethered to scaffolding that held two construction workers.

As the men dangled from the tilting platform, Ben ducked behind the Rustbucket, pressed on the Omnitrix, and became...WILDMUTT!

The workers continued to cling for their lives as the blind dog-like alien from the planet Vulpin used his athletic prowess and hyper-keen senses to make his way toward the distressed laborers.

But before he could reach them...

"Over here! Somebody help!" The plea came from another worker. This one was trapped on the ground inside a burning truck that was pinned beneath a fallen steel girder.

There seemed to be no way that Wildmutt could get to all three men in time.

Then a mysterious young girl wearing a cat-like mask arrived on the scene.

Recognizing the charm hanging from her neck, Grandpa Max cried out, "Gwen? Is that you?"

"I'm Lucky Girl!" the new superhero screamed. "Stay calm!" she reassuringly shouted to the trapped truck driver. The panicked man tried to take her advice.

Looking around, Lucky Girl noticed a wooden board with two smaller pieces of wood on top of it.

As her amulet began to glow, she jumped fearlessly on the end of the wood panel, catapulting one of the pieces of timber through the wayward crane's window, hitting the lever inside, causing it to release a wrecking ball, which plummeted to the ground, landing on the back end of the truck, resulting in the steel girder that trapped the trucker to slingshot toward the red button that controlled the construction elevator!

While the truck driver dove out of his cab right before the vehicle exploded, the elevator quickly shot up the shaft just as Wildmutt was jumping over it to reach the two workers as they struggled to hold on to the scaffolding.

The elevator slammed into Wildmutt, hurtling him into the air.

As Wildmutt plummeted back toward the elevator, he crashed through its floor, causing debris to tumble toward Lucky Girl!

Gwen dived into the front seat of a parked cement truck. In the process, she knocked its stick shift into reverse, causing the vehicle to back into a drainage pipe, which toppled toward Wildmutt as he hung on to the cable. The canine-like alien fell into the cement truck's mixing barrel, covering him with wet cement.

Meanwhile, the toppling drainage pipe stopped, as if by magic, right below the two dangling construction workers.

The workers let go of the scaffolding and dropped through the metal tube onto a discarded mattress.

When Wildmutt finally climbed out of the back of the cement truck, the local media were snapping pictures of Lucky Girl as she proudly asked, "*Who's your hero?!*"

And a new superhero was born!

CHAPTER FOUR:
The Charms of Bezel

Twilight fell as Hex, clutching *The Arcameda Book of Spells*, drifted down the street.

His mind was preoccupied with finding the lost jewel from his magic necklace – without which he would not realize the full power contained in the mystical text.

As he passed a store window, he noticed a display of television sets all tuned to the nightly news. Each showed the face of Lucky Girl. An outside speaker allowed him to hear the program.

"And now," reported the anchor, *"our special interview with New Orleans' newest superhero – Lucky Girl!"*

"How'd you pull off this amazing rescue," the on-scene reporter asked.

"With style, of course!" Gwen responded.

As the camera drew back to reveal Lucky Girl's necklace and charm, Hex's eyes widened.

Meanwhile, back inside the Rustbucket, Gwen looked at her computer screen.

"I cross-referenced *The Arcameda Book of Spells* with dark magical charms. Here's a picture of Lucky Girl's jewel. It's part of a set called the Charms of Bezel. It says here it contains the power of luck. There are other charms with the powers of fire, levitation, and reincarnation."

"Whoa!" Ben said while looking over her shoulder. "Those are the charms Mr. Freak wore at the museum when XLR8 kicked his butt."

"There's more," Gwen continued. "It says that *The Arcameda Book of Spells* contains incantations to be used with the Charms of Bezel and that all the charms must be together for their full power to be accessed."

"So you're keeping this Hex clown from realizing his full potential," Ben teased.

"Hey," Gwen retorted, "his loss is my gain."

"I'm afraid it's more like *was* your gain," Grandpa Max interrupted.

"What do you mean?" Gwen asked.

"I mean we need to return that charm to the museum," Grandpa Max answered.

"Not fair!" Gwen and Ben echoed in unison, surprising each other by their agreement.

They continued, "Not before I..."

"...use it again!" Gwen insisted.

"...try it!" Ben cried.

The two cousins began quarrelling.

"The world needs the power of Lucky Girl!" Gwen declared.

"News flash!" Ben shot back. "*I'm* the only superhero here!"

"Face it, Cousin," Gwen retorted. "You're one of two superheroes now!"

"All the stuff you did at the construction site," Ben argued, "wasn't you! It was that charm!"

"Well, your powers aren't because of *you* either!" she retaliated. "Your powers come from that watch!"

"You're just jealous of me!" Ben shouted.

"Am not!" Gwen answered.

"Are, too!"

At that very moment, a startling news report came in over the radio.

"And in the 'News of the Weird,'" read the

announcer, *"reports are coming in that the city's famed Haunted History Museum has come alive with dozens of visitors trapped inside!"*

"You know that can't be good," Ben said.

"Grandpa, don't you think returning my lucky charm can wait just a little bit?" Gwen said.

"Okay, let's go!" Grandpa Max agreed as he turned the Rustbucket around and headed for the museum.

The sun had set by the time the Tennysons arrived on the scene. The Haunted History Museum was inside an antebellum mansion that had seen better days. It was next to a cemetery that was also run down.

Ben and Grandpa Max exited the Rustbucket and could already hear the shrieks of the visitors inside.

"Which of your Omnitrix heroes are you planning to transform into?" Grandpa Max asked with concern.

Ben looked thoughtfully at his alien watch and responded, "This looks like a job for..."

But before he could complete his sentence, let alone activate the Omnitrix, he was interrupted.

"Back off! I'll handle this!" Gwen declared, now clad as Lucky Girl, confidently jumping out of the RV.

"I'm the real hero here!" Ben screamed.

"We'll see '*who's your hero,*'" Gwen challenged as she raced toward the museum.

"Wait for me!" Ben called, chasing after her as Grandpa Max followed them both.

But unknown to all three, Hex was watching from the museum's upper window.

"Lucky Girl," he laughed to himself, "I've been waiting for you. I knew you couldn't resist my trap."

CHAPTER FIVE:
The Sorcerer's Trap

Ben, Grandpa Max, and Lucky Girl entered the Haunted History Museum.

Up above, a group of five visitors were clinging desperately to a balcony as a mysterious force pulled it loose from the wall.

"Everyone stay calm!" the masked girl shouted. "Lucky Girl is in the haunted museum!"

As Hex watched Lucky Girl run up the staircase en route to the trapped patrons, one of the charms on his necklace began to glow.

Ben, meanwhile, ducked behind a large column and pressed down on the Omnitrix.

"You don't need luck when you've got real superpowers," he bragged as he transformed into… FOUR ARMS!

At the same time, the wobbly staircase collapsed, sending Lucky Girl to the top of a tall pedestal.

While Lucky Girl fought to maintain her balance, the collapsing balcony tilted further, and the museum-goers struggled to hang on.

For one woman, the struggle was too much. She lost her grip and fell toward the ground floor. Fortunately, Grandpa Max was there to catch her. The entire building began to crumble as the balcony separated from the wall. But just as everyone atop the terrace was about to be thrown to their deaths, Four Arms grabbed hold of the last remaining support beam.

"I've got it!" the multi-limbed alien grunted, using all his might to become a literal pillar of the community.

Lucky Girl looked on from atop the teetering pedestal and realized she had to do something fast. Not even Four Arms could hold up that entire balcony forever – and, in any event, the stranded people wouldn't be able to hold on much longer.

As her lucky charm began to glow with increasing intensity, its light reflected off the crystals of the gigantic hanging chandelier.

Was the charm trying to guide her? She decided to take the leap of faith!

Lucky Girl grabbed hold of the dazzling light fixture and swung toward the marooned group. Her feet barely made the terrace as she struggled to keep her grasp of the chandelier.

"Jump on everybody!" Lucky Girl instructed.

The four remaining tourists dove for the light and latched on to it.

As the quintet swung their way to safety, Four Arms finally let go of the balcony support beam, and the terrace itself came crashing down.

Meanwhile, the chandelier stopped swinging, leaving Lucky Girl and the others dangling high above the floor as the fixture dislodged from the ceiling. They all screamed as they fell downward!

Just as they were about to hit the floor, the chandelier cord, which was still attached to the roof, became taut, breaking their fall just in time!

As they all dropped to the floor, a powerful force flung open the museum's doors and began pushing everyone – except Lucky Girl – outside.

Not even Four Arms could resist the incredible fury. When the doors slammed shut, only the masked heroine was left inside.

Lucky Girl looked around and swallowed nervously. Suddenly the large display room became completely silent. And her enemy was invisible.

Then a strange field of circular yellow energy engulfed Lucky Girl's hands. The harder she fought to free herself, the tighter the energy gripped her. Suddenly it began lifting her off her feet and dragging her helplessly upward toward a second-floor promenade where the evil Hex was awaiting his prey.

"Give me my charm!" he demanded.

"You either have it, or you don't!" Lucky Girl retorted to the charmless villain.

Hex, confident of his victory, levitated himself downward. But Lucky Girl would not surrender. She grabbed hold of a velvet drapery and threw the heavy curtain over her pursuer. Disoriented, Hex stumbled into a suit of armor, which keeled over on top of him.

Lucky Girl smiled.

"You know," she suggested, "if you really wanted the charm, you should have said 'please.' Don't they teach you anything in sorcerer school?"

As Hex thrust aside the armor suit, Lucky Girl finally experienced fear as she ran down the darkened hallway. When she reached the end of the corridor, she looked around and realized there was no escape.

Then, as her charm again glowed intensely, the thought crossed her mind that things aren't always as they seem. While there was no visible way out, could there be a hidden way out? Gwen had to find out – fast!

The room grew eerily colder, a terrifying sign that Hex was drawing closer.

With little time left, Lucky Girl continued to survey the library. She noticed that her charm became brighter in certain areas of the room.

When she spotted a bust of the museum's founder, the stone's emerald gleam became almost blinding.

Lucky Girl pulled back the statue's head, revealing a button inside. When she pressed it, a secret passageway opened beneath the mantel.

Gwen stepped inside and nearly stumbled down the twisting stone stairwell. But she continued through the circular tunnel with great intensity as the greatest evil she had ever faced remained in pursuit.

CHAPTER SIX:
When Luck Runs Out

The doors of the museum burst open as Ben, still in the form of Four Arms, and Grandpa Max entered the main building.

"Where'd they go?" Four Arms wondered.

"Judging from the direction of the chilly breeze, I'd guess they went that way," Grandpa Max said, pointing down the dark corridor.

Meanwhile, Hex entered the museum library, where he turned his icy glare toward the entrance to the secret passage.

He looked down into the shadowy stone stairwell and smiled as if he knew Lucky Girl's luck was running out.

Gwen ran, but the tunnel seemed endless, and the mustiness of the air made it hard to breathe. She leaned on the wall, accidentally knocking a stone loose. The sound echoed through the chambers and caused the opening of yet another secret space, this one filled with skeletons that tumbled toward her.

Lucky Girl screamed and tore out of there as fast as she could. But in her fright, she lost her sense of direction and found herself running directly toward Hex!

When Hex saw her, he held up his staff and shouted, *"Interna mobilus!"*

With that, the walls began shaking.

Looking over her shoulder, Lucky Girl knew she couldn't outrun the speeding fiery orb that Hex had sent her way, so she hit the ground. She felt the tingle of concentrated electricity as it whooshed past her and blasted a hole in the wall ahead. The blast also caused a cave-in that dropped stone debris between Hex and Lucky Girl.

Now was her chance to make a break for it!

Lucky Girl ran though the hole created by the energy explosion and realized she was in the cemetery next to the museum. She hid behind a large tree as Hex emerged from the dark hole.

The evil sorcerer, again sensing her fear, began walking toward the masked heroine.

With each step he took, the air around Lucky Girl became colder. The wind also blew round and round with increasing urgency, as if the very intensity of Hex's evil was upsetting nature itself.

Then Hex stopped and looked directly at the tree Lucky Girl was hiding behind. He raised his staff as the fierce wind snapped off her necklace and sent the charm into his hand.

Gwen felt powerless as she watched the evil sorcerer laugh out loud. He arrogantly declared, "Now I possess all the powers of the Arcameda! No force in the universe can stop me now!"

Suddenly, the roots of the tree reached up from beneath the ground and began wrapping themselves around Gwen's ankles.

Gwen fought as hard as she could, but the mighty oak tentacles were just too strong. They wrapped themselves around her until she was completely enveloped in their clutches.

She could no longer even see as the powerful roots covered her eyes and began pulling her into the earth.

Gwen's heart began beating faster and faster

as she considered the stark possibility that Lucky Girl's luck had, indeed, finally run out.

Then came the sound of frantic digging and the wonderful sight of Four Arms ripping apart the roots that bound her.

Grandpa Max reached down into the hole and pulled her to safety.

"Thank you!" Gwen said with total gratitude.

"Where is he?" Four Arms asked.

"There!" Grandpa Max responded, pointing to the hill that looked down on the city.

"This town never appreciated my magic," the vengeful wizard said as he opened *The Arcameda Book of Spells*. "Now I will destroy it."

"*Arava pelotis gallametroy!*" he recited as lightning bolts began striking New Orleans.

"*Sitero Mikora...*" he continued.

But before Hex could complete the incantation, Four Arms leaped at him. They both fell into a stone courtyard. As they got up and faced each other, Gwen and Grandpa Max arrived on the scene, eager to help.

"Stay back!" Four Arms insisted.

Hex rose into the air and landed atop a mausoleum adorned with three winged gargoyles.

"How dare you challenge me!" he thundered from atop the stone tomb.

With pure evil in his eyes, he looked down upon the multi-limbed hero and spouted the words "*Narkela vortium!*" As a fire swirled out from his staff, the gargoyles came to life!

They then flew toward Four Arms, engaging him in a furious three-against-one battle.

Hex, meanwhile, turned his attention back toward the city. He raised his arms and prepared to continue casting his evil spell. But then the sting of a rock to the shin broke his concentration. He turned around and saw...Lucky Girl!

"Luck only takes you so far!" Gwen declared to Grandpa Max as she hurled a second stone. This one hit Hex in the forehead, causing him to lose his balance and fall from the mausoleum to the ground below.

That caught the attention of one of the gargoyles. It angrily flew toward Gwen.

Grandpa Max reached into a pile of debris and lifted a solid steel bar.

"Going...going..." he said to himself, assuming a baseball batter's stance as the gargoyle approached.

"Gone!" he swung the bar with all his might as if it were a bat and smashed the gargoyle to smithereens.

At the same time, Four Arms hurled one of the two remaining gargoyles into the mausoleum's wall, shattering it to bits. He then squared off against the final gargoyle, grabbing it in a multi-limbed bear hug. Tighter and tighter he squeezed, until the stoney menace crumbled into a pile of lifeless dust.

Lucky Girl walked over to the unconscious Hex and ripped the Charms of Bezel from his neck. As she walked away, the evil sorcerer came to. He was about to go after her when he felt the grip of four hands on his shoulders.

He struggled weakly as Four Arms picked him up and threw him into an open tomb. Grandpa Max then sealed Hex's fate as he placed a stone over the crypt.

Now it was Hex's turn to wait in darkness until the police came to take him away.

But in the meantime, Gwen held the Charms of Bezel – and all the power Hex had craved – in her own mortal hands. Thinking out loud about the possibilities, she said, "I could fly, harness electricity, and bring trees to life. The power of the universe could be mine."

Then, pausing for a moment, she concluded, "Or I could just be me."

She placed the magical charms on top of a concrete coffin, picked up a shovel, and smashed them. Blue streams of pure energy flowed upward into the night sky.

Later, back inside the Rustbucket…

"You know, you two made a pretty impressive team. I'd say you're *both* heroes," Grandpa Max said.

"But my powers are gone," Gwen sighed.

"You did the right thing by destroying those charms," Ben said, feeling empathy for his cousin.

"Ben's right," Grandpa Max reassured her.

"I guess," Gwen agreed.

Gwen then looked over at Ben.

"Can I request just *one* favor?" she asked.

"What?" Ben replied

"Maybe," she asked, "you can just admit I did a good job."

Ben looked over at Gwen, took a deep breath, and said, "Gwen, you did a good job."

Gwen smiled.

"Happy now?" Ben asked.

"Totally," she answered.

"Good," Ben replied, "because I'm never saying it again!"

"You don't have to," Gwen said as she pulled out her mini voice recorder and hit the PLAY button.

"Gwen, you did a good job...Gwen, you did a good job..." it repeated over and over again.

"Oh, man!" Ben cried, covering his ears as Lucky Girl got the last laugh.

Ben prepares for action.

Four Arms fights a gargoyle!

Grandpa Max, Lucky Girl, and Four Arms witness an amazing sight!

Lucky Girl saves the day!